# Yummy
# Scrummy

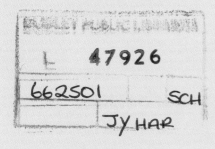
First published 2005
Evans Brothers Limited
2A Portman Mansions
Chiltern Street
London W1U 6NR

British Library Cataloguing in Publication Data

Harrison, Paul
    Yummy Scrummy. - (Twisters)
    1. Children's stories - Pictorial works
    I. Title
    823.9'2 [J]

    ISBN 0 237 52899 1

Printed in China by WKT Company Limited

Series Editor: Nick Turpin
Design: Robert Walster
Production: Jenny Mulvanny
Series Consultant: Gill Matthews

# Yummy Scrummy

Paul Harrison
and Belinda Worsley

Evans

"I'm hungry," said Fly.

"Mmm, pizza.
Yummy scrummy."

"Mmm, chips.
Yummy scrummy."

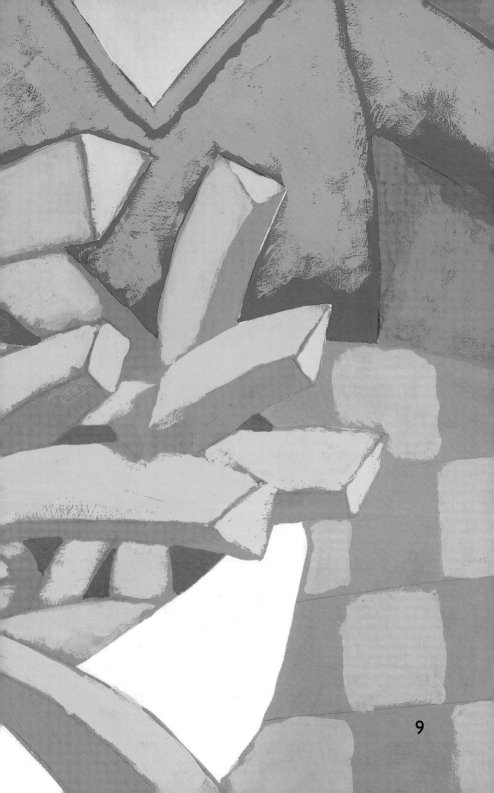

9

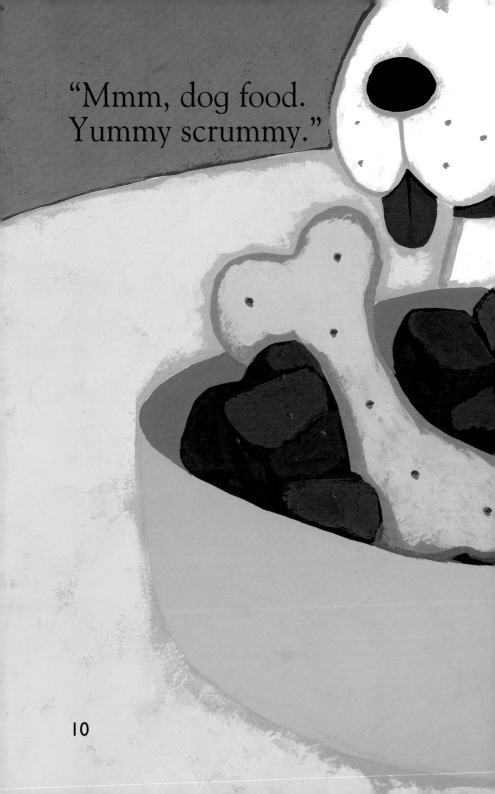

"Mmm, dog food. Yummy scrummy."

"Mmm, crisps.
Yummy scrummy."

12

13

"Mmm, cola.
Yummy scrummy."

14

BURP!

"Time for pudding!"

"Mmm, trifle.
Yummy scrummy."

20

"Mmm, doughnuts.
Yummy scrummy."

27

# THWAP!

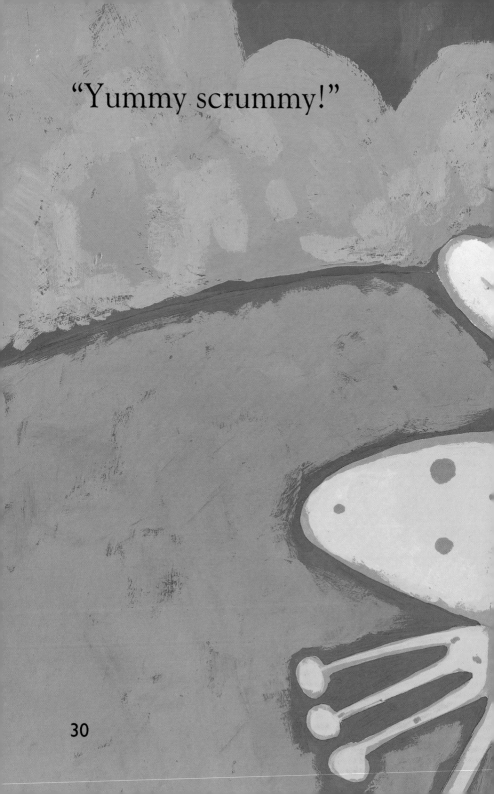

"Yummy scrummy!"

31

Why not try reading another Twisters book?

**Not-so-silly Sausage** by Stella Gurney and Liz Million
ISBN 0 237 52875 4
**Nick's Birthday** by Jane Oliver and Silvia Raga
ISBN 0 237 52896 7
**Out Went Sam** by Nick Turpin and Barbara Nascimbeni
ISBN 0 237 52894 0
**Yummy Scrummy** by Paul Harrison and Belinda Worsley
ISBN 0 237 52876 2
**Squelch!** by Kay Woodward and Stefania Colnaghi
ISBN 0 237 52895 9
**Sally Sails the Seas** by Stella Gurney and Belinda Worsley
ISBN 0 237 52893 2

If you liked Twisters try a ZigZag!

**Dinosaur Planet** by David Orme and Fabiano Fiorin
ISBN 0 237 52793 6
**Tall Tilly** by Jillian Powell and Tim Archbold
ISBN 0 237 52794 4
**Batty Betty's Spells** by Hilary Robinson and Belinda Worsley
ISBN 0 237 52795 2
**The Thirsty Moose** by David Orme and Mike Gordon
ISBN 0 237 52792 8
**The Clumsy Cow** by Julia Moffatt and Lisa Williams
ISBN 0 237 52790 1
**Open Wide!** by Julia Moffatt and Anni Axworthy
ISBN 0 237 52791 X
**Too Small** by Kay Woodward and Deborah van de Leijgraaf
ISBN 0 237 52777 4
**I Wish I Was An Alien** by Vivian French and Lisa Williams
ISBN 0 237 52776 6
**The Disappearing Cheese** by Paul Harrison and Ruth Rivers
ISBN 0 237 52775 8
**Terry the Flying Turtle** by Anna Wilson and Mike Gordon
ISBN 0 237 52774 X
**Pet To School Day** by Hilary Robinson and Tim Archbold
ISBN 0 237 52773 1
**The Cat in the Coat** by Vivian French and Alison Bartlett
ISBN 0 237 52772 3